About the Book

This book was written to help you teach your child about the grace of God. What is grace? How can your child benefit and learn from our Father's grace. Enjoy the pages told through a little girl named "Grace".

Hello, my name is
Grace

I'm here to help you understand what the grace of God is and what that means for you. God is a loving and gracious God. He is kind to us and wants the best for all of us. Even though it is not something we deserve, God sheds His grace on us as a free gift. Another gift from Him among all the other blessings He bestows upon us.

Not only does God graciously justify and forgive us when we do the wrong things, but He continually pours His grace into us. He awards us many blessings and gifts. He finds favor in us. He grants us wisdom, understanding, and knowledge. He even entrusts in us power, to those who believe in Him. He protects us and heals us because He cares for us so much. Having that close relationship with God through His son Jesus, God will always and continually flow His loving grace into our lives.

2 Peter 1:2

Grace and peace be yours in abundance through the knowledge of God and of Jesus our Lord.

The more you learn about who God is and His son Jesus, the more you will be at peace in your life. You will see just how kind and gracious He is. You will want to know more, and your eagerness to learn more will please Him. He will keep showering you with grace and more knowledge.

America, America, God shed His grace on thee.... Do you know that song? "America the Beautiful" What a beautiful song. God sheds His grace on everyone around the world too. We are saved by His loving grace and His beautiful son Jesus. How blessed we are.

This cactus can withstand the mighty power of the sun and the heat of the desert. It can survive with little water, and can protect itself with its hard prickly needles. God created the cactus to be able to overcome such conditions. Just like this cactus, under God's grace, we shall overcome the harsh conditions of sin! We are forever protected under the Son of God!

Each of you should use whatever gift you have received to serve others, as faithful stewards of God's grace in it's various forms.

Titus 2:11

For the grace of God has appeared that offers salvation to all people.

Through the grace of God, we will be saved and protected by God. He will take good care of us here on earth, and give us the gift of everlasting life!

Amazing Grace

So, through God's amazing grace, we are saved. The gospel is all about God's grace through Jesus Christ. In Acts 20:24 Apostle Paul calls it "the gospel of the grace of God" and "the word of His grace"

Let us then approach God's throne of grace with confidence, so that we may receive mercy and find grace to help us in our time of need.

Hebrews 4:16

James 4:6

But He gives us more grace. That is why Scripture says: "God opposes the proud but shows favor to the humble."

God doesn't like it when we boast, brag, or show off. He wants us to do great things but from our hearts and out of our love for Him. We do everything for Him. God gets all of the glory in all that we do. Remember, we cannot do anything without God's grace. All of our gifts and talents and knowledge comes from God. We need to be humble and thankful to Him. Thank You God for everything!

We are not slaves of this world of sin anymore because of God's grace! His grace gives us the power to overcome and defeat the evil one! We are strong in Jesus Christ! May God rain down His beautiful grace upon all of us.... Thank you dear Father in Heaven, You are so good to us.

Ephesians 2:8

For it is by grace you have been saved, through faith, and this is not from yourselves, it is the gift of God.

Reach out and take God's hand my friend. May His grace shine down upon you and give you peace. Your Friend Forever, Grace

About the Author

After losing my husband of 26 years in a motorcycle accident, that's when my walk with Christ began. Never being able to have children God placed it on my heart to adopt. That's when my inspiration for my first children's book began. My gift of artistic ability, and my love of writing made it easy. God made it urgent for me, and my sweet little girl made it fun to write these books. God's timing is always perfect. My first book was "My Life with Faith". The second book to this series was "My Life with Hope". My last book in this series will bring all the little girls together, Faith, Hope, Grace and of course Joy, in "My Life with Joy". I almost gave up on adopting a little girl, it was taking so long. I told God I was going to give up on the idea. At that moment the phone rang.

"We have a little girl perfect for you Carla, her name is Faith". I am blessed by the gift of grace. Please visit my website:

www.carlacarson.com